NO 22 '02	DATE DUE		

DANCING WITH THE INDIANS

DANCING WITH THE INDIANS

by Angela Shelf Medearis   illustrated by Samuel Byrd

Holiday House / New York

Library of Congress Cataloging-in-Publication Data
Medearis, Angela Shelf,
Dancing with the Indians / by Angela Shelf Medearis;
illustrated by Samuel Byrd.
p.   cm.
Summary: While attending a Seminole Indian celebration,
a black family watches and joins in several exciting dances.
ISBN 0-8234-0893-0
[1. Dancing—Fiction. 2. Seminole Indians—Fiction. 3. Indians
of North America—Fiction. 4. Afro-Americans—Fiction. 5. Stories
in rhyme.] I. Byrd, Samuel, ill. II. Title.
PZ8.3.M551155   1991
[E]—dc20   90-28666   CIP   AC
ISBN 0-8234-1023-4 (pbk.)

For Michael and Deanna, with love

A.S.M.

*For my wife, Lois Isley, and my children,
LaTanya, Tamika, Ayana, Taj, Ashley, and Talauren,
whose love and support nurtures and sustains me*

S.B.

This book would not have been possible without the cheerful assistance of
my great-uncle and aunt, Paul and Izilla Davis,
who searched through sixty years of memories
to answer my endless questions and supply me with material.
Also, I'd like to thank my editor, Margery Cuyler, and John Briggs,
both from Holiday House, Inc.
Finally, I'd like to offer a special thanks to my mother, Angeline Davis Shelf,
for telling me about my great-grandfather, John "Papa" Davis,
and his love for the Indians and their customs,
as well as the Indians' love for him.

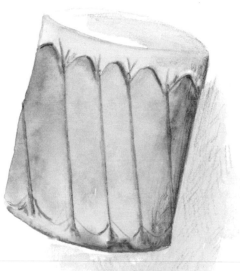

Mama's packed our supper,
the sheep are in their pens,
it's time to go and visit
the Seminole Indians.

Golden threads of sunlight
trickle through the trees
turning leaves above us
into lacy canopies.

We hear about our grandpa,
as our wagon creaks along,
living with the Indians
because slavery was wrong.

He worked on a plantation
before he ran away,
traveling by night,
hiding by day.

Seminoles rescued Grandpa,
making him their friend,
calling him blood brother,
Black and Indian.

Each year we go to visit,
honoring those he knew,
joining in the dancing,
watching what they do.

Our wagon nears the camp.
Drums pound and move our feet.
Soon everyone is swaying
to the tom-tom beat.

The Ribbon Dance is first.
The women gather around.
Shells on wrists and ankles
make a tinkling sound.

Shimmering satin ribbons
float from head to toe,
shining human rainbows
in the firelight's glow.

Moccasins of dancers
make gentle raindrop sounds.
Satin ribbons spin
around, around, around.

The shadows dance in time
to magic music too.
They dip and bow and twirl
as the dancers do.

Soon the Rainbow Dance
comes to a colorful end.
Clapping and whistles are heard
by women, children, men.

The women and their shadows
melt into the dark;
Drummers strike a steady beat.
The rattlesnake dancing starts.

Dancers join their hands.
With every step they take,
they twist and writhe and curl,
the coils of a giant snake.

The slithery animal glides
into the smoky night.
War dancers startle us,
leaping into the light.

Warriors' moccasined feet
make rumbling, thundering sounds,
wheeling, whooping, whirling,
stomping on the ground.

Fiercely painted dancers,
shadows in the flames,
reckless silhouettes,
fearless and untamed.

Warriors stamp and holler,
an angry cavalcade.
I draw away from them,
a little bit afraid.

They sing of ancient battles
gloriously fought and won,
of shaggy buffalo,
and brave deeds they have done.

When the pink of morning dawns,
the warriors dance away.
The drums make friendly sounds.
"Come dance with us," they say.

"Dance the Indian Stomp Dance,
join us one and all."
We move into the circle,
hearing the drummer's call.

Dancing with the Indians,
we dip and stomp and sway.
Dancing with the Indians,
until the break of day.

Dancing with the Indians,
we dance and dance all night.
Dancing with the Indians
in the firelight.

Dancing with the Indians
in the rosy light of dawn,
our morning chores are calling
with the rising of the sun.

Our dance is over now,
but only for the night.
Papa says we're coming back
to dance by firelight.

My great-grandfather, John Davis, escaped from slavery around 1862. He traveled to Okehema, Oklahoma ("Okla" is an Indian word for people and "humma" for red, hence, *Oklahoma* means "red people") when it was still Indian territory. The Seminoles, who were forced to move to Oklahoma from Florida after the Seminole Indian wars, accepted my great-grandfather as a member of their tribe. "Papa" John married a Seminole Indian woman and they had a son, Bunny. That marriage failed. My great-grandfather moved near Oklahoma City and married an African-American woman, Mary Ellen Hawkins, my great-grandmother, around 1909.

Twice a year, Papa John, Mary Ellen, and their nine children, Leo ("Buzzy," my grandfather), Mary, Ethel, Willie, Ederne, Irene, Paul, Freeman, and Oreta traveled to Okehema for the week-long Indian powwow. Papa John joined in the Indians' religious purification ceremonies and dances. Mary Ellen brought her wonderful fried chicken and helped the Indian women prepare the evening feasts. The children played Indian games. After Papa John died, my grandfather, Leo, took my mother, Angeline, and my uncle John to the powwow. Almost 100 years later, many of my Oklahoma relatives still join in the Indian powwows, and they still do the Stomp Dance!

The text for *Dancing with the Indians* was inspired by my ancestors' experience.

Angela Shelf Medearis
January 15, 1991